E
AD

Adler, David A.

I know I'm a witch

$13.45

DATE			
DE 5 '88	JE 12 '90	NO 12 '91	AUG 28 '94
MR 14 '89	JY 23 '90	AG 7 '92	NOV 30 '94
JE 9 '89	AG 16 '90		JUL 13 '95
JY 6 '89	AG 25 '90	SE 28 '92	NOV 6 '95
JY 22 '89	SE 10 '90	OC 22 '92	AUG 17 '96
JY 27 '89	OC 29 '90	JE 7 '93	OCT 17 '96
SE 28 '89	DE 1 '90	AG 17 '93	OCT 13 '97
OC 27 '89		SE 21 '93	DEC 01 '97
NO 16 '89	FE 12 '91	OC 11 '93	OCT 07 '99
MR 15 '90	JY 25 '91	NO 8 '93	NOV 19 '99
	SE 9 '91	DEC 6 '93	JY 19 '00
MY 14 '90		JUL 30 '94	OC 04 '01
			MY 15 '02
			JE 5 '02

© THE BAKER & TAYLOR CO.

I Know I'm a Witch

I Know I'm a Witch

By DAVID A. ADLER

Illustrated by
SUÇIE STEVENSON

Henry Holt and Company · New York

Text copyright © 1988 by David A. Adler
Illustrations copyright © 1988 by Suçie Stevenson
All rights reserved, including the right to reproduce
this book or portions thereof in any form.
Published by Henry Holt and Company, Inc.,
115 West 18th Street, New York, New York 10011.
Published in Canada by Fitzhenry & Whiteside Limited,
195 Allstate Parkway, Markham, Ontario L3R 4T8.

Library of Congress Cataloging-in-Publication Data
Adler, David A.
I know I'm a witch.
Summary: Even though her parents do not believe
she is a witch, a young girl mixes a magic potion
for her nasty Aunt Ruby.
[1. Witches—Fiction] I. Stevenson, Suçie, ill.
II. Title. III. Title: I know I am a witch.
PZ7.A2615Ik 1988   [E]   86-33508
ISBN 0-8050-0427-0

First Edition

Printed in Hong Kong
10 9 8 7 6 5 4 3 2 1

0-8050-0427-0

To Eddie,
a good boy
with a great imagination

I can't fly
but I know I'm a witch.
I know about things before they happen.

This morning,
as soon as I looked at the calendar,
I knew it would be a bad day.
It was Aunt Ruby's birthday.
I would have to visit her.

Aunt Ruby always pinches my cheek
and tells me I'm cute.
And she gives me old cookies to eat.
Witches don't like old cookies.

I have a pointy witch's hat.
I made it from newspaper and cardboard
and painted it black.
I put on the hat
and thought about visiting Aunt Ruby.

I decided to make a witch's brew.
When I drink a brew,
I can make things happen.
I would make rain, thunder, and lightning.
My parents wouldn't take me to Aunt Ruby's
in weather like that.

I went into the kitchen
and I poured some yellow juice,
brown syrup,
and ale of ginger into a glass.
I mixed it well
and watched it bubble.

Then I drank the brew.
It tasted terrible,
just like a witch's brew should taste.
After I drank the brew,
I said some secret witch words
and I knew that soon there would be
rain, thunder, and lightning.

I went to my room
and played with my cat.
She's black, of course.
All witches have black cats.
Her name is Tituba.

Cats don't like rain,
so I told Tituba
not to go outside.

There was a knock on my door.
"That's Dad," I told Tituba.
"He wants to tell me to get ready
to visit Aunt Ruby."

I opened the door.
"We're going to visit Aunt Ruby,"
Dad said,
"so take off that hat
and get ready to go."

I knew he would say that.
That's because I'm a witch,
and a witch knows about things
before they happen.

I took off my hat
and went to the car.
Tituba followed me.
"She can't come along,"
my father said.
"Aunt Ruby doesn't like cats."
I knew he would say that.

While we waited for my mother,
I looked up at the sky.
The sun was shining
but I knew that soon there would be
rain, thunder, and lightning.

I looked at the playground across the street.
Children were on the swings.
Young children were playing in the sandbox.

Too bad, I thought.
When it begins to rain,
all the children will have to run home.
The little children will be frightened
by the thunder and lightning.

I looked at the little children
and decided not to scare them.
I would stop the rain.
Good witches can do that.

I closed my eyes,
made the good witch sign,
and turned around four times.
When I opened my eyes,
the sun was still shining.
I did it!
I had stopped the rain, thunder, and lightning.

Then I thought about Aunt Ruby.
I would give her a potion.

It would make her love cats.
It would make her stop pinching my cheek.
And it would make her serve new cookies,
or ice cream,
or something I like.

"I'll be right back," I told my father.
I ran inside to make the potion.
Colors are very important in potions.
I knew I needed green,
so I opened a can of peas
and poured the juice
into an old peanut jar.
I added ketchup for red,
torn newspaper for white,
and bread crust for brown.
I closed the lid of the jar
and shook it real well.
My potion was ready.

I ran outside.
My father and mother
were waiting for me in the car.
They asked me what I had in the jar.
I told them,
"It's a potion for Aunt Ruby."

"When are you going to stop
this witch nonsense?" my mother asked.

"I knew you would say that,"
I told my mother.
And I did.
That's because a witch knows about things
before they happen.

When we got to Aunt Ruby's
she kissed Mom and Dad.
Before she could pinch my cheek
and tell me I'm cute,
I showed her my potion.
I told her to drink it.

She took the jar
and held it up to the light.
She looked at the potion.

Then she gave it back to me.
She said she wasn't thirsty.

"I'm glad you didn't bring that cat,"
Aunt Ruby said.
Then she pinched my cheek,
said I was cute,
and gave me old, hard cookies to eat.

That's the trouble with a potion.
It doesn't work
if the person doesn't drink it.

I sat and listened
while Mom and Dad talked to Aunt Ruby.

Aunt Ruby said she was real glad
we came to visit.
While they talked, I nibbled on a cookie.

I think it was the same old cookie
I nibbled on the last time we visited.

Aunt Ruby told me
to take some cookies for the ride home.
I took them all.
The next time we visit,
she'll have to give me new cookies.

On the way home
I said that I knew Aunt Ruby
would pinch my cheek
and say I'm cute.

"Don't tell me you knew that
because you're a witch,"
my mother said.
"You knew that because you're smart.
You remember what Aunt Ruby did
the last time we visited."

"That's right," my father said.
"You're just a very smart little girl."

I smiled.
My parents were right.
I am a smart girl.
I'm smart enough . . .

. . . to know I'm a witch.